H🐽gs Back Books

– a nose for a good book ...

Published by
Hogs Back Books
34 Long Street, Devizes
Wiltshire
SN10 1NT
www.hogsbackbooks.com

Printed in Malta by Melita Press
ISBN: 978-1-907432-56-9
British Library Cataloguing-in-Publication Data.
A catalogue record for this book is available from the British Library.
1 3 5 4 2

THE GRANIMAL
CAN GRANIMALS
FLY?

Written by
Christian Alexander
and
illustrated by
Tanya Fenton

The friends of Pug's Hole

SNORK

BEAKY

THE GRANIMAL

PONGO

LITTLE GROMIT

CONTENTS

Chapter One –
The Granimal has landed

Pongo claimed that he had discovered the large mysterious pink egg, which appeared one winter's morning in Pug's hole, on the little grass patch by the willow tree, next to the stream. Snork argued that he had seen it first from high in the sky as he flew overhead. Whoever you believe, one thing is certainly true – Pongo, Snork, Beaky and Little Gromit all helped to hatch the egg and they were all there to welcome the Granimal as he broke out of his shell one hot August afternoon.

Pongo took the Granimal home with him to give him tea. He led him silently along the path to his house. Once inside, he pointed to the armchair that he used for important guests. The Granimal sat down timidly and looked around. Every so often, he put a hand up to his mouth and sucked one of his many fingers.

Pongo stared at the Granimal for a while and then decided that all this finger-sucking must mean that he was hungry. He went to the larder and looked at the shelves. "Now let me see," he muttered, "what would a granimal eat?"

Pongo ate almost anything, and his larder was full of meat, vegetables, nuts, raisins, cereal, strawberry jam and numerous other bits and pieces. Finally, he decided on a bowl of porridge, liberally sprinkled with brown sugar. "Very wholesome," he thought, "for something so small."

"Come and eat, Granimal! You must be hungry," he said, putting the bowl on the table.

The Granimal sat down and watched Pongo intently as he munched his way through his own meal of chopped nuts and raisins. Finally, the Granimal lifted the wooden spoon, scooped up a large helping of porridge and speedily put it into his mouth. At once, a look of great distaste came over his face. He dropped the spoon and shook his head

violently from side to side.

Pongo looked distressed. "Oh dear! You don't like porridge?" he said.

"No, not a bit."

"What would you like instead?"

"I don't know," said the Granimal, quickly sucking a finger. "I don't know what I like."

"Then we must find out," said Pongo, and he went over to a large wooden chest in the corner of the room and drew out a big, black book. On it was written in gold letters: *Concise Oxford English Dictionary*. Pongo had found this book by the path at the edge of the forest, where the school children passed by on their bicycles. After a few days, as no one had claimed it, he took it home. He'd never told anyone about the book as he liked to look up long words in it and impress his friends with his knowledge.

Pongo put the book on the floor and nosed through the pages: "grain—granary—granite—", but there was no mention of the word "granimal", let alone what one might eat.

All this time, the Granimal sat very still, his eyes growing larger and more doleful. Pongo closed the book and shook his head sadly. He walked back to the larder and stared at the shelves. From the topmost corner, a gleam caught his eye. He pulled up a stool and peered in. There, next to a box of biscuits, was a large tin with the words "Rice Pudding" written on it.

Pongo brought it down, put the rice pudding in a bowl and waited for the Granimal to try it. This time the Granimal's mouth spread into a huge smile, and without further ado he polished off half the tin.

"Thank goodness for that!"

said Pongo. "Now we can go to bed, and tomorrow we'll try to find you somewhere to live."

Pongo fetched a pillow and the Granimal, full of rice pudding, curled into a little ball and quickly fell asleep. Pongo looked down at him for a while, amazed by how small and strange he looked. Then, shaking his head, he climbed into his own bed and shut his eyes.

Chapter Two – Staple diet

Pongo and the Granimal both woke up early the next morning. Pongo had his usual bowl of cereal, while the Granimal ate the rest of the rice pudding, which Pongo had mixed with a little strawberry jam.

Pongo cleared away the dishes and then announced, "We'll go to Snork's house this morning. He and I are the cleverest animals in Pug's Hole, and between us we'll think of a place for you to live."

"Thank you," said the Granimal. And after a short pause added, "May I have some more rice pudding please?"

"I'm afraid it's all gone," said Pongo, peering deep inside the tin. "Never mind, I'm sure Snork will have some for you."

The Granimal looked pleased, and Pongo noticed that when he was happy his eyes became slightly moist and shone a brighter green.

So they set off, walking side by side along the path towards the big oak tree, where Snork lived. As they went, they sang, with Pongo bellowing the deep notes and the Granimal joining in with the high-pitched, twiddly bits. Soon, they arrived at Snork's tree house, where Pongo banged on the door.

High up a window opened, and

Snork leaned out. "Whatever you want, go away!" he shouted.

"Come down!" called Pongo. "We've come about an important matter."

Snork climbed out of the window and glided to the ground. "What's all the fuss about?" he said crossly. "It's much too early for visitors."

"Good morning, Snork. Do you have any rice pudding?" asked the Granimal.

"What?" said Snork.

"Have you any rice pudding?" repeated the Granimal. "Perhaps with a little strawberry jam?"

"What on earth for?" said Snork.

"Breakfast," said the Granimal.

"It's what he eats," explained

13

Pongo, nodding his head wisely. Then he added (having looked up the word in the *Concise Oxford English Dictionary*), "In fact, it's a granimal's staple diet."

Snork didn't know what "staple diet" meant, but didn't like to ask in case he appeared foolish. He paused for a moment and said, "I don't have any staple diet, but I do have a few tins of rice pudding if you can make do with that?"

The Granimal's eyes turned bright green. "Oh thank you, Snork!" he said.

Pongo and the Granimal went in through the wooden door in the trunk of the tree and climbed up the little staircase to Snork's home, while Snork flew back in through the window. He brought out a tin of rice pudding and put it on the table.

"What about the strawberry jam?" asked the Granimal.

"I'm afraid that's all gone. Will raspberry do?"

"I don't know," said the Granimal, "but I'll try it."

Snork put a small dollop of jam and the rice pudding into a bowl and the Granimal sat down and enjoyed his second breakfast; the raspberry jam was every bit as good as the strawberry.

Chapter Three – Flight or fright?

Pongo settled himself in one of Snork's armchairs. "Here's the problem," he said, "we must find somewhere for the Granimal to live. He can stay with me for a while, of course, but eventually he'll need his own home."

"Where he can keep his own tins of rice pudding," said Snork, seeing the tin rapidly empty. "Don't worry, I know a good tree quite near here."

"A tree?" said Pongo. "What do you mean? Granimals don't live in trees!"

Snork put on a large pair of spectacles. He'd found them some years ago and thought they made him look very clever, highly important and extremely dignified. He drew himself up to his full height and peered through them at a rather blurred Pongo. "And why not? Birds usually live in trees," he said.

"But the Granimal isn't a bird!" said Pongo. "He's a sort of a—kind of a—well—he's just a granimal."

"He came out of an egg, didn't he? So he must be a bird," said Snork firmly.

Pongo didn't know what to say.

It was true, the Granimal had come out of an egg, but he had a strong feeling that he couldn't be a bird. He walked over to the Granimal and looked him up and down. "He doesn't have any wings," he said finally.

"Look carefully," said Snork.

Pongo and Snork walked round and round a rather dazed Granimal and poked him now and again.

"There you are, definitely no wings," said Pongo.

Snork was forced to take off his spectacles. He peered closely at the Granimal, but there wasn't even the smallest of wings to be seen. "I'm sure they're there somewhere," he said, "folded up inside. They'll appear when he begins to fly."

"Absolute rubbish!" snorted Pongo.

"Not at all," said Snork. "Come on, Granimal, let's see what you can do! Let's see you fly! Look, like this."

Snork spread his wings and, flapping them hard, rose up into the air a couple of feet, before settling gracefully down again.

The Granimal's eyes grew very large, and he sucked hard on his fingers.

"Come on!" said Snork. "You'll never learn unless you try."

The Granimal took his fingers out of his mouth and waved his spindly arms up and down. Nothing happened.

"There you are," said Pongo,

"no wings and no flying."

"Not yet," said Snork. "It takes a little time to get the hang of it. Come along, Granimal, let's go and practise!"

So off they marched down the stairs, out of the tree house and along the forest path. Pongo followed a little way behind, muttering to himself.

Soon, they came to an old oak tree in the middle of a clearing. It had huge branches that reached to the sky, and even the lowest of these was a long way from the ground.

"Here you are, Granimal," said Snork, "just the place for your new home."

The Granimal looked up at the huge tree with its high branches.

Suddenly, he felt very small and very frightened and wished he were somewhere else.

"How do I get up there?" he asked timidly.

"Quite easily," said Snork. "Just fly onto that big branch. Beaky and I will hollow out some of the trunk to make you a nice place to sleep, and when you want to come down, you can glide to the ground."

"Oh," replied the Granimal, feeling very unhappy. He tried flapping his arms up and down and taking little jumps, as Snork had shown him, but he couldn't rise more than a few inches in the air.

"Never mind," said Snork, "getting up is always the most difficult part. Climb onto my back and I'll get you started."

The Granimal climbed onto Snork's back and clung tightly to his neck. With some difficulty and a great deal of flapping, Snork finally reached the lowest branch, where the Granimal slid off.

"There," said Snork, "that was easy, wasn't it? Now you can glide down."

The Granimal looked at the ground far below. He could see Pongo staring up with a worried look on his face.

"I'll just wait a while to get used to things, so that I feel more at home when I fly back up again," he said. "You go first, Snork, and I'll follow."

Snork spread his wings and flew down to rejoin Pongo on the ground. Together they looked up at the Granimal. All they could see was a tiny, terrified face peering over the edge of the branch.

"Glide down!" shouted Snork. "It's quite easy once you start."

Pongo said nothing. He felt sure the Granimal was not a bird, but couldn't come up with a good reason why a thing that came out of an egg might not necessarily fly.

"Glide, glide, glide!" shouted Snork.

The Granimal was now very frightened indeed. "Granimals can fly," he kept saying to himself, "they can."

At last, he stood on the edge of the branch, closed his eyes tightly, pushed several fingers into his mouth, gave a little cry and jumped off. After a fraction

of a second, the Granimal knew there was no way he could fly.

Snork, looking up and seeing the Granimal hurtling towards him, suddenly realised he was not a bird. And Pongo knew he'd been right all along.

With a loud thump, the Granimal landed on Snork's feathery wings, squashing him to the ground.

"Ouch!" shouted Snork.

The Granimal opened his eyes. When he realised that he wasn't hurt, he stood up and smiled.

"Did I do it right, Snork? It was kind of you to catch me. Shall we try it again?"

"No, I don't think you're quite ready yet," Snork groaned, struggling to his feet. "Perhaps you should begin with a house on the ground, until your wings have grown. I think I'll go home to rest for a while. My back is a little sore." And with that, he hobbled off down the path.

"Well," said Pongo, "at least we now know that granimals can't fly!"

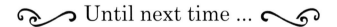 Until next time …

Look out for other titles in the Granimal series